THE GHOST TRAIN
DEMON

To Jack,
Glad you enjoyed it!!

A. Newton

THE GHOST TRAIN
DEMON

ADAM NEWTON

authorHOUSE®

AuthorHouse™
1663 Liberty Drive
Bloomington, IN 47403
www.authorhouse.com
Phone: 1-800-839-8640

Published by AuthorHouse   03/12/2013

ISBN: 978-1-4817-8736-9 (sc)
ISBN: 978-1-4817-8741-3 (e)

CONTENTS

Chapter 1

PETTY SQUABBLES

Friday night, school finished just over five hours ago and a group of friends from the local secondary school have met up to go to the travelling carnival that had visited town. There were five in the group, each person was different in many ways and came from all sorts of backgrounds, this was what made them appreciate their friendship so much, and no one definitely passed any unwanted judgments. They all stuck with each other and supported each other, even in the hardest of times. Tonight would be the ultimate test for this bond.

It was just after nine thirty in the evening, and the autumn air was chilly, yet fresh. The night had begun to close in the hour beforehand, and the cloudless sky gave an almost uninterrupted view of the canvas of stars sparkling above them. The carnival itself wasn't too big but was good enough to entertain the whole of the local area. The local park, large and oval in shape, was situated in the suburbs and was surrounded on all sides by black metal fencing with arrows atop each of the spokes, intersected by brick columns. On the outside a road ran the entire circumference of the park, flanked by trees and street lamps. Residential streets branched off from the park in different directions. There were four entrances to the park, located directly opposite each other, connected to each other by clean, brick paths that crossed in the centre of the park around a small fountain, which was only ever turned on during the summer months. The carnival itself was set up in the eastern half of the park, and even before they had entered the park through the opposing entrance, they could hear the sound of the music and the people enjoying themselves, and they could feel the warm, welcoming glow of the lights, spewing an attractive aurora around the surrounding houses.

"Mate, I can-not wait to get some fairground hot dogs inside me. "I-am-starving" Announced Dave. Dave was considered a city boy, with a slight cockney accent. He wore faded jeans, a baggy Tottenham Hotspur football shirt, white trainers and a black Nike baseball cap. He had an unpredictable mood, particularly with people he didn't know; otherwise he was happy around his friends.

"You're always starving! And the fact that you only ate a few hours ago just makes it sound even more pathetic!" countered Nick. Nick was an average lad, he had no interest in fashion and simply wore what made him feel comfortable; jeans, combat trousers, t-shirts, whatever, and he certainly didn't let anyone pass any unwanted judgments about his personal likes and dislikes. Tonight he had gone with basic dark jeans, a t-shirt he had bought on a family trip to see the D-day beaches in Normandy, and a pair of grey casual trainers.

"Yeah, but it wasn't much of a filling 'dinner,'" he replied, twitching his fingers as he said 'dinner'. "Besides that was more of an afternoon snack than an actual dinner."

"Alright", sighed Garth, "we'll stop off at a burger bar, but only after we've been on some of the rides. I don't want you throwing your guts all over me". Garth was a quiet lad, but whenever he spoke, he put a smile on his friends' faces, no matter what mood they were in. He was very well-built, very handsome with a shaved and smoothly defined face; he had well groomed hair and always wore clothes that looked so perfect he could have been a top model, if he'd wanted too. He wore smart white trainers, slightly faded denim jeans, and a very non-creased, tight t-shirt, and despite having practically every girl in the school chasing after him, he was still single—which didn't surprise his friends in the slightest—as he was still looking out for the one girl who was perfect for him.

"I tell you now; there will be no one who can beat me at the rifle range. I don't even care if those rifles aren't zeroed properly, I'm not gonna miss a single one of those targets. Do any of you *dare* challenge the master of marksmanship?" This was an offer from James that John definitely couldn't refuse, not this time. The last time John had challenged James at the rifle stand he'd had his butt severely whooped, by the end of the competition James had completely cleared his targets while John was still trying to knock down his pyramid of cans. From then, John's pentathlon training had become more intense and he had become an amazing shot with a firearm.

"Yes! I'll give you a run for your money this time." announced John with a fiery glare of confidence "I, John, challenge you, James, to a shootout at the rifle range, five pellets say I'll kick your pompous ass!"

"Five? I only need one! You're on, mate!" James said, shaking John's hand.

James was considered by most as a farmer boy, he had a country accent, wore tweed or leather shoes and coats, wool or even cashmere jumpers, shirts of various colours, jeans or cords. He was a generally nice person who always spoke what he thought. He had a wide rough face, with a constantly determined look on his face. He was definitely going into agriculture when he was older. John was a keen sportsman, and was on the brink of becoming an international pent athlete for the Great Britain, currently ranked second in the UK and Ireland. He was fairly small and skinny due to his dedication to sport, and he was the type of person who could eat all the junk fast food restaurants had to offer and not put any weight on. He had a slim face, patches of facial hair and a few spots. Everything about him was sporting, black and dark blue running shoes, baggy tracksuit trousers and cotton Umbro t-shirt. He wasn't born in England, but to an American family that had moved over just after his birth. Still, he retained a strong American accent.

"Fiver says I'll whoop your ass," John started.

"Fiver!? I'll raise you a tenner, mate!" James finished.

"As you wish, Jimbo! Prepare to be humiliated!"

"I just can't wait to have a go on the merry-go-round…" Nick said. Everyone in the group just stopped where they were and just stared at Nick, the expressions on their faces saying, *you what . . . ?* "Guys, just kidding!" Nick said, trying to dig his way out of it.

"Yeah, yeah, sure . . ." the others muttered as they started walking again.

"No seriously, I'm just messing with you!"

"Look, if that's the sort of thing that floats your boat then that's fine with us." said Dave reassuring Nick sarcastically.

"You can all go to hell . . ." Nick muttered light heartedly under his breath, the others just chuckled.

A few minutes later they were in the bustling centre of the carnival; all sorts of colours were being thrown at them over a blanket of yellow sparkling light. James and John had just paid for their five shots each on the air rifle range; five shots to knock down a pyramid of cans. They both loaded their first pellet and closed the breach. They took their aim as their friends watched intently. James was the first to pull the trigger. He was aiming at the left pyramid, the outside of the bottom centre can. Direct hit! The can came out from under the pyramid. The pyramid itself tumbled down, taking with it one of the other cans on the bottom, but simply pushing the other one slightly to the side. He proceeded to reload. John squeezed his trigger, aiming at the top of the central can on the bottom tier, just on the side. It spun from underneath the pyramid, causing it to crash underneath its own weight, all over the shelf. He placed the rifle, breach open, down onto the table and folded his arms, a smug grin covered his face while Dave, Garth and Nick whooped and laughed both in amazement and delight. James looked at John open mouthed, and then gave him the biggest evil look he had ever given anyone. He took out a ten pound note and slapped it into John's open hand before taking his second shot, completely missing the last can on his shelf. The Dave, Garth and Nick howled with laughter while John still stood where he was, maintaining a smug look on his. He put his rifle down without even bothering to take another shot at the remaining can, gave John one last glance, then walked off, muttering "you're buying my food, pal." The others followed, mocking him.

They went round the rest of the carnival enjoying the other attractions on offer to them, with James having a mock grudge against John; they each drove their own vehicle in the bumper car arena, giggling loudly as each hard crash knocked more air out of their lungs. Dave and Garth went on a couple of throwing games, trying to win a cuddly toy. Neither of them was very successful in their attempts. They walked past the merry-go-round, mocking Nick as they went by, stopping every so often to offer him an extra chance to 'go enjoy himself'. Dave had his fill of a hot dog, a burger, two portions of chips and even some candy floss and a toffee apple; after all of which he still complained he was hungry and kept stealing everybody else's chips when they weren't looking. He got caught by John as he nicked a chip, John responded in kind, reaching across to steal a chip off Dave's polystyrene plate—only to be fended off by a sharp stab on the hand by Dave's little wooden fork, and a menacing glare. John's reaction was of silent bewilderment.

"I'm not sitting next to *you* on the next ride ..." Garth uttered, having witnessed the amount of food Dave was consuming. At one point they smiled and winked at a group of girls as they walked by, who smiled and waved coyly back at the boys, giggling amongst themselves. They headed to the *Hall of Mirrors*, where they had great fun running full pelt into mirror after mirror they simply hadn't seen. Nick was first to finish and laughed hysterically at the others as each one went face first into another mirror, mouthing *shut up* and *go away*, embarrassed when they realised he was watching them. They got their just desserts when they exited to find Nick had suffered a bleeding nose from running into mirrors one too many times.

CHAPTER 2

∽⁕∾

THE RIDE

THE LAST RIDE they came to of the night was the ghost train. It looked just a cheaply enjoyable at all the other attractions, with roughly painted artwork of a zombie and Frankenstein's monster, light bulbs thinly painted green and purple and the painted words *Haunted House* poorly painted to look like blood. The ticket booth was set to one side. It didn't look very big from the outside; roughly thirty or so metres wide, ten high—including the headboard with Frankenstein and a zombie—and around another seven meters going back.

"Bet this ain't scary at all," said Dave.

"Yeah, you'll be covering your eyes the second we get in there! You always do with things like this!" mocked Garth, they all chuckled.

"Yeah, shut up . . ." was all Dave had to come back with.

They all handed a ticket in to the man behind the counter and got onto a cart. The bars came down.

"There's no escape from me this time, Garth!" Dave laughed crazily in Garth's face as he sat down next to him.

The cart moved off into the tunnel. Although they were still moving, it was still pitch black, and it remained pitch black for a good five minutes or so. All of a sudden they turned a tight corner and came out into what looked like a bleak set-piece, on their right was a curved walled, coloured like a head stone, that looked like it was taken straight out of a station on the London Underground, there were poster frames, but no posters in them, they just had the familiar JCDeceaux at the bottom of the frames. There were also one or two Underground signs, but no name, they were just blank, not even in the traditional red and blue of the London public transport system, just two shades of grey. On their left hand side, where the platform should be, was a small grass field, more like a front lawn, with a single concrete track leading ten metres or so to a small, old looking, forties style two story house. There were no lights on. A single tree stood just the left of the house in full bloom, although the atmosphere just made it look lifeless with grey leaves and bark that looked like it had thick layers of grey paint covering it. The whole place was very dull; the sky was dark and cloudy, almost stormy. A cold breeze blew gently around the place. The grass, waving ever so slightly in the breeze, had the only colour in the place, although it was still very pale green. It seemed like a real place in a horror movie, although through the atmosphere they could still make out the borders of a room. Even the boys' clothes looked dull and grey. Their skin looked pale too.

The cart trundled slowly to the middle of the 'station'. The bars lifted. All five lads sat where they were in dead silence for another five minutes. It was James who broke the deathly silence;

"I don't get it! What the hell happens now? Does this thing go off again or are we meant to get out and have a wander?" he was now growing extremely impatient. "This has never happened on either of the other times we've been on this ride before, the past few times we could actually tell how much the skeletons and ghosts were falling apart!"

"I've no idea, let's see what happens when we get out . . ." answered John.

"It doesn't make sense anyway, on the outside it looks nowhere near as big as this, it's just a little, rectangular cabin . . . It definitely wouldn't fit something like this inside it," Nick said, pointing out the logics of it all. "Although it does seem oddly real."

They all climbed out of the cart onto the pavement and stood around for a few minutes. They then started off towards the house. The second they set off they heard a noise behind them. They spun around to see the bars of the cart had snapped down and the cart itself sped out of the room. The boys just stared in bewilderment. They stood around for another few minutes, waiting for something to happen. Nothing did happen, other than the breeze had started to make them all feel cold. They turned around and focused their attention on the house.

"That was strange," confirmed John with an obvious tone in his voice.

"Not as strange as the attendant who took our ticket, did you see him? He takes our tickets in complete silence, doesn't even tell us where to go, when to get on or even point out some of the safety stuff they normally do," Garth pointed out; "not to mention his face, it just looked so *blank*! Staring straight through us, it was almost like he was possessed!" he finished half sarcastically.

"Yeah, sure, possessed!" replied James, with sarcasm injected into every word. He was still annoyed with the complete novelty of this so-called ride, as well as his embarrassing loss to John on the rifle range earlier on.

They got to the door with Nick in the lead, he stopped at the door and knocked, rasping three times.

"Hello? Anybody in there?" He shouted none-too-seriously for a reply. He got no reply, so he turned around to see what the others wanted to do.

"Let's just see if it's open," said Garth.

"I'll go with that," agreed James.

"Me too," Dave entered.

"Yeah, let's do it, I'm cold!" Added John.

"Alright! But on your heads be it if we actually disturb someone ..." Nick gave in and reached out for the doorknob. As soon as he touched it he sharply withdrew his hand with a short, sharp gasp.

"What's up, Nick?" questioned Dave.

"The doorknob's absolutely freezing!" He whimpered, putting his hand straight into his pocket to get warm.

"Stand aside, wuss!" James burst through impatiently, quickly reaching out and grabbing the doorknob. He too quickly retracted his hand, yelping in pain.

"What's that about wuss, mate?" Nick countered sarcastically, smirking.

"Shut up! You said it was 'absolutely freezing'!" James was furious.

"It was. Look, my hand's still blue and I've even had it in my pocket for long enough now." Nick showed his hand quickly before putting it back into his pocket.

"Well it felt red hot to me!" He was really unimpressed right now; "look at my hand, it's redder than a tomato!"

"Erm . . . guys! Look at the doorknob!" Garth interrupted loudly. The handle itself was glowing red with the intense heat being given off.

"THIS MAKES NO SENSE!" James exploded.

"It really doesn't," John agreed.

"So what are we gonna do now then, Einstein?!"

"I don't know, but your screaming in my face is definitely not gonna make matters any better for us!"

"You got an answer for everythin' don't you, you f-"
James had to be held back by Garth, Dave and Nick as he
made a hostile move against John.

"James! What's wrong with you?! You know he's
right! There's nothing he can do, nothing you can do, and
nothing any of us can do unless we try to make some
kind of sense out of it! Please James, just try to calm
down." James relaxed a little and Garth released him. He
apologised briefly to John. "Still, while we're here . . ."
Garth turned and reached out, positioning his hands two
centimetres away from the doorknob, warming his hands
up. The others chuckled and joined in, excluding James,
who simply had to rub his red hot hand with his cold
hand. This luxury only lasted a brief minute before the
doorknob went cold again.

A moment later they heard a noise behind them.
They wheeled round to see a cart full of girls slide slowly
along the track. They had walked straight past these same
girls earlier, on the way to the Hall of Mirrors. They were
screaming as though they were experiencing the real ride
the Ghost Train was host to. They were. They girls were
experiencing the real thing, the ride the boys *should* have
been experiencing themselves. They could not see what
the boys were seeing, or even the boys themselves. They
playfully screamed at what was possibly another ghost,
or skeleton popping out at them from alternating sides
of the track. The boys looked at each other briefly in
confusion. They started running in the direction of the
cart full of girls, shouting and waving their arms. The

girls must have heard them because they started to look around in blind confusion. The cart all of a sudden picked up speed and rushed off to the other end of the track. The girls simply screamed in delight, completely forgetting about the random voices. The cart sped out of the far doors. The doors closed and locked themselves, leaving the room once again in complete silence.

The boys climbed down onto the track and started trying to push the doors open. They would not budge a single millimetre, even with the full weight of five grown teenage boys pushing and throwing themselves against it. Behind them they heard the entrance doors open and something speeding along the track, they turned to see an empty cart hurtling toward them at break-neck speed with no sign of deceleration. The doors at the far end snapped shut behind it.

"Get onto the platform, quick! Go, go, go, MOVE!" ushered Nick quickly. The five boys quickly scrambled onto the platform. The cart shot past them. It narrowly missed Dave's foot as he just got out of the way in time.

The boys quickly got to their feet, checking themselves over for injuries, and then checking up on each other. They were now stood on the grassy part of the 'platform'.

They heard from somewhere on the other side of the path a faint crumbling noise. They looked to see the ground tearing itself up, something was coming towards them under the ground, a low growling noise emitting from it. The even stranger thing was that the ground was healing itself up after the creature had moved on, as though it hadn't been disturbed at all.

"Get onto the path!" Garth ordered, quickly analyzing what was happening. They didn't need telling twice. They all raced to the path, reaching it just as the creature was preparing to strike. It even revealed part of its flesh to the boys. It looked like some sort of snake, yet with much tougher, bonier, and more ridged skin. As soon as the boys touched the concrete the beast disappeared. The ground healed up after it, as though it had been nicely preserved.

"What the hell was that?!" exclaimed James, breathless and weak from two sudden rushes of adrenaline.

"This place actually wants to kill us!" added Dave.

"I don't know what that was or even where the hell we are, but I think we should head indoors, it seems like our last and only option!" Garth took charge.

"I think so too," John agreed with Garth. All the others could do was to simply nod at each other in agreement, before heading off together towards the house once again, being more cautious than they had ever been in their entire lives.

CHAPTER 3

ᏀᎳᎳᎾ

THE HOUSE

W HEN THEY REACHED the house James cautiously reached out for the brass doorknob again. It felt cold this time, naturally cold.

He turned it slowly and pushed . . .

"Oh, for Pete's sake!"

"What?"

"It's only flippin' locked!" James yelled, banging the door with his fist.

"I say we kick the door down," suggested Nick. "We can't exactly open it normally, and we can't get out of this place. We can't risk walking onto the grass to break a window. It seems to me like it's our only option."

"It might seem like a pretty barbaric thing to do, breaking into someone's house, but I agree with James, it does actually seem to be our only option." John sided with James. The others had no grounds on which to make an argument; they were all in the same boat, and they knew it.

"Ok, any volunteers to kick this thing down?" James asked, at the same time highlighting the door with his thumb.

"Yeah, I'll do it." Dave announced, confidently stepping forward. "Come on then, out the way, let me have a crack at it."

James and Dave stepped carefully around each other on the narrow path, trying not to step on the grass. The rest of boys took a few steps back just to give Dave some room. Dave quickly analysed the door, then focused his attention on the area just below the doorknob. He shifted his position around, trying the get into the best position in which the strike the door, at the same time being able to exert the maximum amount of strength he could possibly give.

"In your own time mate, it's a bit nippy out here!" James pressured, growing impatient once again.

"Oh, shut up! Just give me a minute or two, will you?! Plus you probably didn't even want to do it yourself!"

"Yeah, less talking, more doing. And hurry up with it."

After a few more seconds of testing his foot position on the door, he cracked his knuckles. Lifted his right foot, and summoned all of his strength into his leg. He shifted his weight forward slightly. And sharply kicked the door with his heel, straight on target in the area below the doorknob. The door easily gave way, as though there was nothing holding it shut in the first place. It swung into the house and slammed loudly against the adjacent wall. Dave strolled casually into the house.

"Just be careful, Dave. Before you blindly wander into anything that's potentially life threatening."

"Like what, Nick?"

"I don't know! Just be careful, if this place is trying to kill us out here we might just encounter something, or some things, inside that wants the same thing from us."

"I agree, Dave." added John, "Just be careful."

Dave carried on in, in front of him was a hallway roughly two metres wide, with a staircase on the right hand side leading straight up to the next floor. The hallway lead straight along the length of the house, to what must only have been the back door, with two doors located on the left hand wall, both of which were closed.

"Hey! Shall we go straight up or stay down for now?" Dave asked the rest of the group.

"I say we check out what's down here first, just in case." John spoke.

"Just in case of what?!"

"I don't know! Just, let's go. Ok?"

"Ok . . ." Dave said with a sigh.

They approached the first door on the ground floor. Dave opened it and they stepped into what they assumed to be, or must have been, the living room. It was bare, and very basic. There were a couple of book shelves around the sides, both of which were empty. There was a tatty looking sofa in the middle facing an empty fireplace in the opposite wall. The left wall held the window that looked out to the front of the house, and to the underground tunnel. A couple of tatty looking armchairs flanked the old sofa, which itself was stood on top of an old, plain brown rug with no real colour to it. The right hand wall had bookshelves stood up against it, near the far wall, and a door that led to the next room.

Garth was the first to sum it all up; "How barren is this? It's so . . . Bare!"

"You're not wrong, mate. But we couldn't have expected a mansion or something, after outside we're sure not getting any luxuries in here!" John chuckled.

"Well even so . . . Whoever it is that owns this place really needs to put at least some colour in here."

Dave made a move towards the other door in the room, next to where they were stood. The others followed, still looking at the room around them. Dave turned the doorknob and opened the door. It led them into the kitchen. It was a typical looking kitchen with skirting boards leading round the edges with a series of drawers and cupboards underneath, with a second series of cupboards above the skirting boards. A basic wooden table sat in the centre of the room with a set of four similarly wooden chairs set equally around it. A metal sink and draining board was situated in front of the window, which itself looked out the back of the house to the rearmost wall of the host building; the sink and taps themselves were completely clean and looked as though they were completely new fittings. There was a door on the right side of the room which would just lead them back to the hallway. There were no other doors in the room, no doors that lead outside. The boys all entered the room and stood around the table and chairs, looking around to see if there was any sign of life in the house. James started opening cupboards and drawers, with no regard to how much noise he was making. It didn't really matter; there was nothing in any of the drawers, or cupboards. It was all empty. All of the materials felt very real though; marble counters, wooden table and chairs, metal sink and draining board. Garth turned one of the taps on the sink. To his surprise there was water pouring out of it. It was crystal clear and definitely inviting. But Garth knew better and turned the tap off. As soon as he had done so the basin became bone dry, as if there hadn't been a drop of water land in it for a long time.

"I don't get it . . ." James said.

"What's not to get, James? We've just seen absolutely nothing outside, we're definitely not expecting to see anything inside. Did you really expect this place to be furnished with antiques?" Garth laughed.

"Well . . . I would have thought there would have been more life to it than this. Is this even part of the ride?

I certainly don't remember any rides I've ever been on like this. It could be a haunted house, but there's nothing here that could be scary." James replied disappointedly.

"Well at least it looks well preserved, just look at how shiny the sink looks, especially for a place like this." Nick joined in.

After a brief silence and a further look around the ground floor of the house, they decided to take a look upstairs. They trumped up the narrow staircase together with no thought as to how noisy they were being. The staircase itself was bare wood, which simply rose straight up to the next floor. When they got to the top of the stairs the found it in a similar, if not the same, as the floor below. At the top of the stairs, directly above where the back door would be downstairs, was a window. Turning around, at the other end of the landing, above where the front door was, was another window next to a second staircase leading up above the first, that inevitably led up to an attic room. The landing itself had two closed doors attached to the right hand wall, again just like the floor below.

The five boys moved cautiously towards the first door. James slowly reached out and turned the doorknob. The scene on the other side was like something out of an X-rated horror movie. Blood stained the walls, the ceiling, the window, the furniture and the door. There was not a single item or area that hadn't had blood spewed all over it. There was a corpse on the floor in between the bed and the wall. It had been hacked into pieces, which was now scattered all around the torso. Another corpse lay on the bed, as though whoever it was had been killed in their sleep. The head, which had been decapitated, was on the floor on the other side of the bed, and one of the arms lay separated on the opposite side of the bed to the body. It was impossible to know what colour the bed sheets had originally been, as the whole bed was brown from where it had been completely covered in now dried blood. James screamed in absolute horror and recoiled out from the room, crashing into the banister across the hall, and still staring, shell-shocked, into the room in front of him. The others rushed past one by one to see for themselves what had spooked James so much. They each gasped as they witnessed the scene. After a few moments they all backed out, and John, the last to exit, closed the door slowly behind him.

"What, or who the hell did that!?" James yelled.

"I don't know. But I think it's about time we found a way out of th-"

They heard a creaking noise coming from the floor upstairs.

"Sounds like we've disturbed someone . . . Or something . . ." John whispered to Nick.

The creaking turned into heavy footsteps. The footsteps moved slowly towards the top of the second staircase. James edged forward slightly. The others followed at a distance. The footsteps started to climb down the stairs. As the footsteps drew nearer to the bottom, the boys could see a silhouette. No one moved, rooted to the spot. It reached the bottom of the staircase, and turned towards them. It appeared to be, or what looked to them, like a very well built fireman. It clothes were all black, burnt and charred with not a single other colour. The helmet and visor were both black as well, the visor itself was tinted, but the soot and burnt plastic made things look much worse. The heavy boots and coveralls looked like they were severely burnt and melted in places. It carried a blunt-looking fireman's axe in its right hand.

"Oh . . . I'm so sorry sir—we didn't mean to break in—we didn't know where else to go or-" James' stuttering was cut short when the strange figure gave a long deep growl, moving slowly towards James. It raised its axe over its shoulder. James slowly started to back away, trembling with fear.

"Ok I'm really sorry, we'll just be leav-" He was cut short again. Only this time the strange being swung it's axe down and swiped James' head clean from his neck. Blood spattered the wall, the ceiling, the demon and the boys

The others all froze in complete shock and horror as the thing stepped towards them again, raising its axe. All they could do was slowly shuffle back into a corner and watch as it came toward them and swing its axe again. This time it was Nick in the firing line, who received the same predicament as James. The remaining three stood ready to move, they just needed a motive, and a very quick decision as to which way to go. Do they go through the horror room to their right and jump out the window onto the grass, with the risk of injury, or even worse, being attacked by the thing that lived in the grass? Or do they try to avoid the slowly encroaching being that just murdered their friends, by going down the empty staircase and trying to find a way out? They were given a definite motive, and an involuntary decision; for next to them, on the other side of the bedroom door, came loud scratching noises. The corpses were alive and trying to break the door down to get them. It was all the motivation they needed, and legged it. The being swung it's axe down at John, who was the last to start off down the staircase. He ducked, so low he almost tumbled down the stairs. The being's axe gave John a clean trim off the top of his hair. The legs of all three boys were pumped full with pure fear, taking them down stairs three at a time, and straight out through the front door, which was still wide open from when they came in. John threw the door shut behind him, hoping to delay the demon's pursuit by at least a few precious seconds while they would try to find a way out. As they had gone through the door they caught a brief glance at a plaque next to the door they had all completely missed earlier. It read:

Whoever Should Wake
The Sleeping Demon
Shall Pay With Their Lives,
and all who stands in the way!

So that was what the being was. A demon. They had woken a sleeping demon. They realised as they approached the edge of the platform that it was repeated of one of the advertising boards opposite the platform. This time it was written in blood. As were the names of all the boys, along with two others, which they assumed, must have been the names of the two corpses they had heard come alive earlier.

Just as they were getting desperate a cart sped into the room and stopped at the end of the path, raising its bars. The three boys looked at each other, wondering whether or not to trust it. Behind them came a crashing sound. They turned in horror as they saw the demon simply walk through the door, wood splinters flew everywhere. The demon continued to march slowly toward them, axe clamped tightly in hand. The boys had no alternative than to trust the cart that was still waiting for them at the end of the path. They all ran towards it. Not even slowing to get in, they simply jumped or fell in at full speed. Having briefly righted themselves they sat and waited for the cart to move off. It didn't move at all, even while the demon continued towards them, getting ever closer with every wasted second.

"MOVE IT!!" They all screamed continuously at the cart with ever more fear and panic in their voices. Garth had a sudden subconscious reaction, and quickly closed the bars around them as a last ditch attempt to get the cart moving. The cart moved off. Just as the demon had approached within a metre from the cart. Garth looked back through painfully swelling tears to see the demon watch after them as they exited the room. The doors immediately slammed shut behind them.

Chapter 4

๛

DEATH'S PURSUIT

THE CART BROUGHT the boys back out onto the original entry platform they had used earlier when they first came aboard as a squad of five. They all breathed a sigh of relief. There was definitely one major problem the trio noticed when they emerged; it was deathly quiet. There was nobody left in the carnival. A car moved on the roads surrounding the park, but there was definitely no obvious signs that there was anyone around.

"What time do you make it, Dave?" Garth asked after a brief silence, through tears and a large lump in his throat. As soon as the bars lifted they stepped out, weak at the knees from the exhausted adrenaline. Dave lifted a weakened, quivering arm to his face.

"It's half one, according to my watch."

All they could do with their remaining energy was to climb down from the platform. They looked around, through tears, trying to rearrange their minds and figure out what to do next. Dave slumped to the ground, resting against one of the posts elevating the platform. Garth joined him. So many questions spun round in their heads, making them all nauseous. Had they really woken a sleeping demon? Had they really just seen two of their best friends get murdered in cold blood? Why had they been chosen to wake it? Had they even been chosen, or were they in completely the wrong place at the wrong time? What could they do? Where would they go next? Would anyone even believe anything came out with? They couldn't go to the police. They simply wouldn't believe their story. So that was already a couple of questions answered.

John stepped down from the platform and approached the ticket booth to the ride, hoping to find some sort of clue that might in any way help them. Dave and Garth watched on, still sat against the platform. He looked through the window. Empty. He tried the door. Two bolts were locked in place by padlocks, and John simply didn't have the energy and the tools to open it. He decided to leave it be and return to Garth and Dave.

"Anything?" Dave asked.

"Nothing ..." John trailed off as he saw five silhouettes approach them from across the park. Garth and Dave turned to see what John's gaze was fixed on.

As the silhouettes approached, the boys realised they were the five girls they had seen enjoying the ride while they had been trapped in their nightmare. Dave and Garth got up as the girls got within a few metres of the boys, before coming to a stop.

"What have *you* been up to?!" One of the girls spoke out, using a mixture of sarcasm and part repulsion, having seen the boys looking so worn out and dirty, covered in what looked to them like a mixture of dried red and brown paint. She was mid height wearing pair of tight, light blue jeans, a small strap top and a beige woolen cardigan, with worn out trainers. Her hair was predominantly brown, with a few random streaks of blonde, and a crucifix hung loosely from her neck. "It's a bit late to be painting, isn't it? Or did your spray cans burst all over you?" She chuckled sarcastically.

"Yeah, you look like somebody's died! We didn't disturb you from anything did we?" Another agreed, this time in a friendlier tone.

"Yeah . . . You could say that . . . Probably a good thing, though." was all Garth had to reply; his face simply couldn't hide the pain, and the trauma he had just received. The girls looked at each other like they had stumbled across a bunch of weirdo's.

"So, what are you doing here at this time of night?" The first girl asked.

"Just got off the ride." John replied timidly, not really knowing what exactly he should say.

"Yeah, sure. We followed you on about four hours ago and you're saying you just got off? And where's the other two that were with you?"

"Yeah, we kind of guessed you were after us; we saw you enjoying yourselves on the ride. Might sound weird but we were trying to get your attention by shouting at you." Garth said honestly.

"I remember that, actually!" It was a different girl that had spoken. "I heard someone shouting, it sounded too weird to be part of the ride, so I thought nothing of it . . ."

"Yeah, the rest of us heard it too, so we all decided to sneak out and take a look. Ok, it was more of a dare to see if we were brave enough to enter the spooky house 'if we dared', and to see if it really was haunted. Kind of silly, I know, but here we are!" Another said, jumping on the spot and clapping her hands. She was clearly the most eccentric member of the group. "I'm Stacey. This is Chantelle," she said pointing to the first girl who had spoken, who waved at them sarcastically. "That's Jenny," she said, indicating the second girl who had spoken. Jenny was roughly the same height as Chantelle and wore dark blue jeans, red and white Converse trainers and a dark green cotton cardigan on top of a t-shirt sporting a picture of Jacob from the *Twilight* films. "Over here we got Anna." Anna was the tallest of everyone there, towering over everybody else. She gave a nice *hello* and little wave. She spoke with a slight Russian accent and tonight she was wearing black jeans, black trainers and a navy blue hoodie. "And this is Laura." She pointed to the last girl, who simply smiled and nodded. Laura had long blonde hair and was wearing a plain white t-shirt, light blue jeans and scruffy white trainers.

"I'm Garth. This is Dave . . . and John." Garth indicated briefly.

A brief silence followed.

"So, yeah. Where are the other two?" Alicia asked again.

"Dead."

"Dead? Wha'-how . . . ? May I ask?"

"You wouldn't believe us." Garth looked away.

"Well you look like you've got a good story to tell, just by looking at you!"

He looked away briefly and took a long breath. Just as he turned back to tell them, they heard a series of loud cracking noises coming from the ghost train ride. They all turned to see the exit door on the track burst into pieces and the demon emerge. It had broken out from it's tomb to seek revenge on the rest of the boys for disturbing his sleep! The boys' hearts dropped like boulders when they saw the demon emerge. It picked up a cart that was blocking its path and tossed it effortlessly of the ride.

"We have to get away from it now!" Dave yelled with a small feeling of responsibility inside. The adrenaline had come back and it was time to flee. The boys didn't need telling twice, but it took the girls a couple of seconds to get up to speed with the boys and started chasing after them.

"Who's that!?" Jenny shouted in bewilderment at Dave, who had just forced her to run, which wasn't her most favourite hobby in the whole wide world. Stacey was in tears already, although she didn't quite know why.

"*That* is a demon, and *that's* what killed our friends!" Garth replied. He drew his mobile phone from his pocket and tried to give it some life. It was showing an empty battery. "Dammit! My phone's dead!" Without thinking, Laura pulled hers from her pocket.

"Here! Use mine!" She shouted as she threw it. Dave turned around in time to catch it perfectly. He flipped the top of the phone up and dialed 999. By now they had sprinted out of the park and down one of the housing estates that led away from the park. The operator picked up on the other end.

"Emergency services, which branch do you need, please?"

"Police!" Dave shouted impatiently as he spun around at a T-junction to see the demon still following them at the park end of the street. Where they were, they were semi-bathed in street light, compared to the street they had just come down, which was fully lit.

"Police, how may we help?" Dave hesitated, thinking of what to say. Surely a desperate call about a being chased by an axe wielding demon would be considered a prank call on the police end, and would end up with them getting arrested for wasting valuable police time.

"We need help! We're being chased by a masked murderer with an axe! We're currently where Johnson Street joins Stewart's Street and we would really appreciate any help you could send us. Please help us!" The policewoman on the end of the phone could sense the panic in his voice and responded immediately.

"We're sending a patrol car to your location. Are you able to stay where you are until they arrive?"

"I think so. Please hurry!"

"Ok. Our patrol car will keep us informed." The operator hung up. Dave handed Laura's phone back to her.

"Thank you." He turned to speak to all the girls. "It's us he's after. All of you go home and be safe. While you can." The girls stood still, some looking at the boys, the others at the demon. "Now!" Dave yelled, making them accept the fact that they needed to get out of there. Fast.

"Let's hope we bump into each other soon." Chantelle said, giving Dave a quick good luck hug before turning to catch up with the other girls. The boys turned to see the demon had already come half way down Johnson Street. The boys crossed the junction to the path on the adjacent street. They were at the top of the T-junction. As they faced down Johnson Street. To the right of them Stewart's Street ended in another T-junction, going onto a fairly busy main road, even at this time of night. To the left, the street was another seven hundred metres long, with another T-junction at the end, a turn off was located five hundred metres away that led onto Brazing

Street. As they reached the top of the T-junction, a police Vauxhall Astra patrol car pulled up to them and two officers climbed out and approached the boys.

"What's going on then? Was it you who called about a murderer?" The first officer spoke to them with a Yorkshire accent.

"He's right behind you!" Garth replied with such panic the two officers spun around to see the demon nearing the end of Johnson Street. The second officer confidently approached the 'murderer', expecting some sort of hoax. He then saw the huge blood soaked axe in the demon's hand and spattered overalls, and immediately became more professional

"Halt! Lay down your weapon!" The demon kept coming. It wouldn't have done anything if the officer hadn't been stood between the demon and its target. "Stop! I order you to stop!"

The Demon reached the police officer. It carried on forward as it swung it's axe up from it's side. The officer still had his arm out in a 'halt' gesture. The demon's swing trajectory chopped off the officers outstretched arm a split second before it swiped off his head. The officer didn't even have any luxury of time to react.

The first officer instantly ran to the patrol car and radioed the local police headquarters.

"This is PC Richard Smart, my colleague has been killed and I need armed support on Stewart's street immediately!" He yelled into the radio's microphone. The reply from HQ was instant.

"Understood PC Smart, help is on the way." Police HQ replied. "You'll have company in just a few minutes, hold on tight."

"It'll have to do. I have three-" He was cut short when the demon reached the car and flung it into the air. PC Smart was still holding the radio when the car was thrown away, and he himself was thrown to the ground in front of the demon. He turned over to see the demon raise its axe above it's head. He rolled as the demon swung down, narrowly avoiding the same fate his colleague suffered. The demon's axe became buried in the concrete with a very loud *clang*. He got up as fast as he could and started to run down the street, while the demon struggled to free its axe from the ground.

"With me, lads! We need to leave!" The boys turned and followed, running alongside PC Smart. The local police HQ was alive with activity; officers were getting prepared in the equipment room with a mixture of firearms and riot gear, three armoured vans were being readied in the garage, and a police Twin Squirrel helicopter crew had already scrambled and were taking off. The helicopter had state-of-the-art night vision and thermal imagery to help them keep track of the situation.

"So who is that? Who's just murdered my partner?!" PC Smart demanded through panted breaths.

"That is a demon. Somehow we woke it. It also killed two of our best friends in the same way it killed your partner. We don't know how to stop it, and it seems hell-bent on killing us." Garth replied, panting even more so than PC Smart. PC Smart decided there was enough conviction in Garth's voice, and chose not to argue. "However I think we should see if there are any paranormal weirdoes we can talk to." The demon followed at its standard lumbering walk. Even though PC Smart and the boys were gaining ground, it knew where they, and would not abandon its relentless pursuit until had killed those that had woken it.

PC Smart reached into his trouser pocket and pulled out his personal mobile phone; a new iPhone 5, and fingered the display screen for a few seconds before lifting it to his ear. They were currently just over half way between the two junctions. The demon was only fifty or so metres from Johnson Street.

Just as PC Smart and the boys were approaching the turnoff into Brazing Street, the first police van thundered round the corner, lights flashing and sirens blazing. It screeched to a halt in front of PC Smart and the boys. The siren stopped and the rear doors opened and six officers emerged; three officers—two men, one woman—with riot helmets, shields, riot batons and a Taser gun, which had only recently been introduced to the local police force. When the trigger was pulled, two electrodes fired from the end and embedded themselves into whomever it was aimed at, delivering fifty thousand volts, enough to bring a fully grown adult to the ground. It was also a very effective melee weapon if the situation required it.

The other three police were equipped with full body armour, helmets and weapons, each officer wielding a

Heckler & Koch G36C 5.56millimetre assault rifle and a holstered Sig Sauer P226 pistol. The drivers climbed out, toting their own armour, holstered pistol, and carrying a Heckler & Koch MP5 9millimetre sub-machine gun.

The riot police stopped an equal distance between the demon and the police van, one of which raised their Taser gun.

"Halt! This is your final warning! Give up and surrender!"

The police chopper hovered above, thumping madly against the air to stay airborne. It was closely monitoring every move of the engagement, and relaying all important information back to HQ. Another police van had stopped at the very far end of Stewart's Street—a further two hundred metres away from the Johnson Street junction—and a police sniper team was already laid out on the ground armed with an Accuracy International L96 sniper rifle, the same model as used by military snipers. They were busy analysing everything they needed to take a decent shot if the need arose. Distance to target, wind speed, etc. PC Smart took the boys round the back for cover, while he kitted himself up with spare armour and a pistol. The demon approached the riot police. Residents in the surrounding households had been woken by the noise and had gone to their windows or had come out of their homes to see what was happening.

"Please go back into your homes!" Came a tannoy announcement from one of the vans; some locals did as they were told, some stayed were they were. Another police van and a patrol car had pulled up next to the other and armed police climbed out to join the other armed police officers. The press had also arrived, and had parked up behind the line of police vans. The journalists were being kept at bay by the officers who had arrived in the patrol car.

"Stay here, boys, I'll come back when it's ok."

"Yes sir. Is there any way we can help?" John asked.

"No. Just sit tight right there for me. Is that Ok?"

"Yes sir." PC Smart turned and went back to the front of the van just in time to see the riot policeman with the tazer gun squeeze the trigger. The Taser gave a sharp crack, and the two electrodes embedded themselves into the demon's right shoulder and right abdominal area. The electricity was enough to make the demon flinch violently, but it eventually shrugged it off. It raised its axe. The riot police raised their shields as it swung down. The axe, although it looked blunt, sliced straight through the shield of the centre riot policeman, went through his helmet and became embedded in his head. The other riot police, having realised the situation, leaped out the way while the murdered policeman crumpled to the floor.

"Police, how can we help?"

"This is PC Smart again. I need you to get in contact with a paranormal expert and give them my number!" He shouted to the operator before hanging up and raising his pistol. The demon was only one hundred metres away now.

"Open fire!" The armed police had just been given the order to fire by their commanding officer. Nine assault rifles, four sub-machine guns and a pistol loudly disturbed the night silence, clattering until the clips were spent. The demon was slowly forced back by the sheer weight of the bullets. The bullets were certainly making contact but they were having no effect on the demon, there wasn't even blood coming out of the wounds. Dave, Garth and John were watching everything unfold, the police struggling against a determined foe. The demon continued forward

The firearms officers reloaded while the two remaining riot officers rapidly dropped their shields and charged the demon, hoping it was at least weak enough for them to bring to the ground. They were wrong. The first officer approached the demon on its right side, baton raised. The officer swung his baton into the demon's back. The demon lashed out with a sturdy fist, hitting the officer square in the chest, cracking some of his ribs as he flew back to the pavement. He knocked his head against a tree and became unconscious. The other officer arrived at the left side the demon a second after the other officer had been punched into unconsciousness. All the demon had to do was execute a quick swipe with the axe and take off the officer's raised hand. She screamed in dire agony as she fell to the floor, clutching the bleeding stump that was her wrist.

"Fire." The sniper's spotter said into his ear. The rifle cracked loudly. At first—where the action was all happening—the demon lurched forward as a large calibre bullet slammed through the back of its head and out through the front. Flames erupted from both holes. The demon staggered on the spot before turning around and hurling its axe in the direction of the sniper team. The throw seemed effortless for the demon, especially when the object is being thrown accurately over seven hundred metres. The sniper team saw the axe coming and split quickly to avoid being hit. The axe hit the ground with a loud, metallic *crack* exactly where the sniper himself had been led down just a second beforehand. It slid, screeching along the tarmac, until it came to a stop, becoming embedded in the pavement opposite their junction. The demon turned back to face the firing squad as they raised their weapons again.

Suddenly PC Smart got a phone call.

"Hello, PC Smart," he shouted into the receiver for an answer.

"Hello again PC Smart, sorry to have kept you so long, I'm putting you through to a paranormal expert." The phone clicked and for a second before a new voice came up. The demon was now less than fifty metres away from the firing squad.

"How can I be of assistance?" Came a voice that sounded like a college nerd. PC Smart decided he didn't trust him, but he had no other option but to.

"Hi, I am PC Smart and I'm being chased by an axe wielding demon and I really need a way to stop it."

"OK sir, first of all-" The so-called expert was cut off as the phone clicked over to a new voice, one that sounded more confident too.

"PC Richard Smart, I am part of an organisation that has many years of experience in this field and I need you to tell me everything, so I can tell you what you're dealing with."

"How do you know my name and what is this company of yours?" PC Smart demanded.

"Please sir, from the sound of things you're not in the position to be asking questions. I need answers so I can help you." PC Smart hesitated, glancing briefly at the demon. Dave, Garth and John were eavesdropping, trying to find out what was happening.

"Fine," PC Smart gave in. "I don't know much myself, so I'm gonna hand you over to someone who does." He turned towards the boys as another order came to fire. Another loud burst of rifle fire spoilt the night. The boys were starting to get cold. The demon kept coming after another set of magazines had been emptied. The commanding police officer gave the order to retreat. Everyone got back into their designated vans. The press decided to scarper too. The police vans turned and sped away as fast as they could to the end of the street, turning different directions at the end, before stopping again twenty meters each way from the junction. Garth had been explaining everything to the man on the other end of the phone.

"It sounds to me, that you are the only people that can stop it."

"Us? How? We don't know what to do, much less how!" Garth replied, getting desperate for an answer.

"You are the demon's adversary, the people who disturbed it from its sleep, and subsequently released it from its tomb; therefore you are the only people to offer it a worthy testament, to beg it to stop its rampage. If you fail and are killed, there will be no one else to stop it, and it will simply carry on killing." PC Smart had been rummaging through the van and found a spare pistol and two spare assault rifles. He issued a weapon each to the boys, with one magazine each. The boys suddenly got the message.

"It's all on you now guys. I'll get the police in the other van to clear out. I'll accompany you out of this van and assist you where I can. We'll wait until it comes out of the junction. The officers from each of the vans were already out of foot, blocking the road from other road users. PC Smart and the boys climbed out.

"Do you know how to use these?" PC Smart asked. The boys hesitantly nodded.

"We play video games." John said casually, taking the safety catch off his pistol and cocking it. Dave and Garth did likewise with their assault rifles. PC Smart nodded, impressed.

"I need you to clear the area, fall back and cordon off the street further down." PC Smart said through his radio to the police team on the other side of the junction. The officers hesitated for a second before doing what they were told.

The demon emerged from the junction. The boys turned and raised their weapons. There was a faint whiz from behind the demon and another large caliber bullet slammed through it's back and out through its chest. The sniper team had quickly gathered again and fired another shot. The demon lurched forward again. It regained its balance and turned towards the boys who were waiting for it.

"Do you have a good aim on it?" PC Smart asked loudly.

"Yep." Came a similar response from each of them.

"Fire!"

The boys squeezed their triggers. A single shot came from John's pistol, while a long burst came from Dave and Garth's assault rifles. The recoil made them miss every shot, except for John, whose bullet made contact with the demon's arm. It recoiled. A small flame erupted from the bullet wound.

"Switch to single fire if you can't handle the recoil!" PC Smart shouted. Dave and Garth did as they were told. They each fired again and again. One trigger pull for one bullet until the magazines were empty. The sharp bangs continued, the shots being much more accurate this time. The demon was definitely being affected by the bullets. It appeared weaker, falling down onto one knee. Bullet holes pierced its arms and torso, flames billowed from very one of them. John's pistol was the first to run dry, the cocking slide locked into the open position after the last bullet was ejected. He took one look at it before lowering his arm, turning to the others.

"I'm out!" He announced. Dave and Garth finished at the same time. They both looked into their weapons' ejection ports. Yep, Dave's was out of ammo. However, Garth had received a stoppage. A bullet had failed to eject properly, blocking the next bullet from being fed into the chamber. He quickly handed it to PC Smart. His training kicked in instantly, he applied the safety catch, removed the magazine and pulled the working parts to the rear, locking them in place. He then cleared the obstruction and looked at the magazine. One bullet left. He slid the magazine back into the rifle, and then released the working parts, loading the last bullet into the rifle. He flicked the fire mode selector switch from safety to single shot, and handed it back to Garth. The demon slowly got back onto its feet and shifted towards the boys.

"Ok, buddy, you've got one bullet left, make it count. Aim for the head." PC Smart suggested.

Garth nodded and raised his weapon, peering down the sights. Time seemed to slow as he lined up the front aiming pin with the dead center of the rear aiming loop, and the same with the demon's forehead. He took a big breathe and held it. Moments passed before anything happened. John, Dave and PC Smart stood stock still, staring at Garth, waiting for something to happen.

Garth squeezed the trigger. The rifle exploded, thumping into Garth's shoulder one last time. The firing mechanism stayed open, waiting for a new magazine to feed it with bullets. Garth allowed himself to breathe. The bullet hit exactly where Garth, and the others, had wanted it to. The demon's head was thrown back and it crashed to the ground, lifeless. That was it. It was all over. Garth lowered his weapon and gave a huge sigh of relief. As soon as Garth had lowered his weapon, the demon exploded. The flames went high before they sank into the ground. The tarmac healed itself over, returning to its original state. A moment later they heard a huge explosion not too far away. The three boys now turned their thoughts back to their dead friends, as they handed their weapons back to PC Smart; and what would happen now, now that it was all over.

CHAPTER 5

OPERATION: COVER UP

GARTH, DAVE AND John were taken, via police van, to the park where their ordeal had started. It was now around ten minutes past six in the morning, and the sun was bringing with it a tranquil, light blue tinted sky over the horizon towards them. They got out from the van to see a middle aged man, somewhere in his late forties. He had greying, dark brown hair, and a styled, bushy beard, also going grey. He wore a rough looking grey suit, with brown leather elbow patches, and polished brown leather shoes. When he spoke, he spoke with a deep, soft, comforting voice they recognized from somewhere.

"Good morning, boys." He opened with. "I'm sorry to hear of your predicament, but I hope the information I provided helped you resolve it."

Behind him stood the fairground, including the Ghost Train Ride, which was currently having the last flames put out by the fire brigade.

"Who are you?" John asked straight away. He had been through too much to be shy about anything. "Who do you work for and how did you know how to help us?"

"I am not allowed to tell my name, I can tell you I work for a secret Government team created for this specific purpose, the name of that team I am not at liberty to reveal. I have been in this field of expertise for many years, after having an experience very similar to your own. I know you have many questions which I cannot answer right now. Here's my card, call me if you feel the need for specialist counseling, or if you have any queries about what happened tonight." At this he turned and started walking away. He paused briefly, and turned to face the boys again. "Oh, and good job with that demon." He turned back one last time and carried on walking away.

"Sorry lads, I have to return to the station a.s.a.p. I'll be in touch." PC Smart said, shaking their hands one at a time.

"Thank you for everything." Garth replied softly.

After they waved PC Smart off, they turned in the direction of the carnival. The Fire brigade had finished putting out the fire and had retrieved the charred bodies of four people. As the boys approached, the fireman in charge came to meet them.

"I have been informed to ask you three to identify two of the bodies." He said in a scowling manner. "Follow me please." They followed him to the four bodies, now lying in a row together, removed from the scene of the fire. It only took a matter of seconds for the boys, their faces once again streaming with silent tears, to identify their friends.

"That's James and that's Nick." Dave informed.

"Thank you lads, you can go now." The fireman said ignorantly waving them off. They backed up and turned around to find a man wearing a crisp black suit, waiting for them by a polished black car.

"I need you to come with me; we need to have a chat." He said as he opened the rear passenger door of the car. The fireman watched as they headed silently to the car.

John, Dave and Garth were taken to the local police station, where the mystery man who had driven them there opened their doors and led them inside. No one had spoken a word on the journey; no introduction, no discussion, no questions about where they were going, no nothing. Just an awkward silence.

They were led through the building, none of the police staff even looked at them. They passed a door that was slightly ajar, peering in as they passed they caught a glimpse of PC Smart being spoken to by a disembodied voice. The boys were curious earlier, now they were worried. They were showed through a single door, which felt like it was located at the very furthest end of the station. It was a briefing room, with school-style single desks with chairs, arranged in a block formation facing a virtual whiteboard.

"Please, take a seat." The man said, turning on the light. He spoke in a friendly, yet still professional manner. Once the boys had sat down together near the front, the man spoke.

"I know you don't want to be here right now; and I know you have been through quite a lot in just a small space of time, but I just need to go through just a couple of issues with you, then you are free to go." He paused for a moment, offering them a chance to speak. They sat ready to receive the next round of information, so the man carried on. "Ok, first of all, like I said you've been through a lot tonight, so here's a card with a phone number and details of our specialist psychologist, if you find you're having trouble concentrating, or simply need some advice, or feel the need to book a session with the psychologist, etcetera etcetera; give them a call. Sessions are held here, free of charge at your convenience. Secondly, we will help to organise and fund the funerals of your two friends who were lost their lives tonight." The three boys all boiled slightly with anger that he didn't show enough respect to their dead friends to use their names, but reminded themselves that this man didn't know their friends names in the first place. "You did well tonight, boys. I dread to think what would have ensued had you failed."

He reassured them. "And lastly . . ." The man picked up three sheets of paper from the desk he was leaning on, and handed one each to the boys. Reaching into his pocket, he pulled out a pen and handed it to John. "But most importantly, you will not mention anything about tonight to anyone, anywhere, at any time, and on any method of communication. Nobody must know about what happened tonight—"

"Why not?" Dave interrupted, slightly confused, and a bit annoyed.

"You are not at liberty to ask that question." The man now spoke menacingly, with a cold, oppressive look in his eyes. "If we hear of you talking about this, or telling people about us, you will be sent to a maximum security prison for a long, long time. Do you understand me?" The boys just nodded. It was the only thing they could do. "Now please sign along the dotted line at the bottom of you pieces of paper; this way it is in writing that you have accepted our terms and conditions." One at a time, the boys signed their sheets, each of them feeling oppressed by the anonymous man in front of them, and the organization he represented.

"Fantastic!" The man said cheerily, standing up. He collected in their papers, and they were done. "Up you get then. Follow me." He led them back the way they had been brought in their way into the building and out through the door. There was a car waiting for them outside. The driver opened the door for them to get in. They were finally going home.

Back at the carnival site, a fireman was busy reeling in the last hose, while the rest of his team waited in the cabin for him to finish. From somewhere near the burned out ride, he heard a faint crumbling noise. He looked to see the ground tearing itself up, something was travelling away from the ride under the ground, a low growling noise emitted from it. The even stranger thing was that the ground was healing itself up after the creature had moved on, as though it hadn't been disturbed at all. The fireman shook his head in disbelief, and carried on reeling in the hose.

AUTHOR BIO

⟨⟩

I WAS BORN 7ᵀᴴ April 1989, as the second son, and last
child of a Royal Air Force pilot, a dedicated housewife,
and an older brother; two years ahead of myself. My father's
last post with the Royal Air Force was commanding RAF
Northolt, which is where Royal Flight is based, and had the
very interesting task of greeting Her Majesty the Queen
whenever she travel in, or out of the UK. Unfortunately
he died from cancer just three days before my sixteenth
birthday, but continues to be my idol, and inspiration for
success. My mother, Maureen, now works as a receptionist
in a hospital in Marlborough, Wiltshire. My brother is a
primary school teacher in Burbage, Wiltshire.

I myself am currently employed by Wiltshire Council as a lifeguard at their Marlborough Leisure Centre; where I have gained many achievements, most particularly the lives I have actively saved both in and out of work. I currently live in a village called Kintbury, located near Hungerford in Berkshire, with my wife Chantelle, and our dog Pru, who is a young cross breed between Alsatian and (we think) either golden Labrador, or Staffordshire Terrier. My hobbies and interests include; making models, military history, the armed services, science fiction, and basketball.

My idea for this book actually stemmed from my days at boarding school, where, one night at night time, one of my room-mates forced me to come up with a story so my voice could carry him (and subsequently myself) to sleep, and so I decided to write it down, and release it as my debut book.